DATE DUE		
F CUT	OCT 17 '86 OCT 1 4 2016	
V OCT 31 '73 OCT 21 '82		
JAN 16 '74 DEC 14 '8		
OCT 22 '74 FEB 1 8 1987		
F 2 OCT 19 '94		
JAN 31 '75 NOV 0 3 '94		
FEB 2 0 '75		
OCT 22 '79 3		
MAY 17 '79 4		
NOV 1 0 19 OCT 2 2		
NOV 29 '79 OCT 2 9 1996		

FIC
PRE

Preston, Edna Mitchell
    One dark night; illus. by Kurt Werth.
New York, Viking, 1969.
    unp. illus. col. draws.

1. Halloween-Stories I. Title

9401737

Sneakery Squeekery . . .

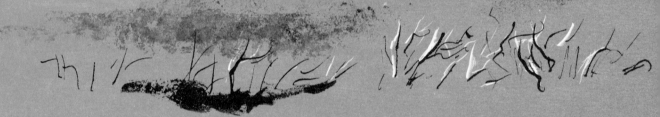

One Dark Night

EDNA MITCHELL PRESTON

Illustrated by Kurt Werth

The Viking Press   *New York*

OTHER BOOKS BY EDNA MITCHELL PRESTON

Monkey in the Jungle, ILLUSTRATED BY CLEMENT HURD

The Temper Tantrum Book, ILLUSTRATED BY RAINEY BENNETT

Toolittle, ILLUSTRATED BY JOE SERVELLO

Pop Corn and Ma Goodness, ILLUSTRATED BY ROBERT ANDREW PARKER

The Boy Who Could Make Things, ILLUSTRATED BY LEONARD KESSLER

Text copyright © 1969 by Edna Mitchell Preston. Illustrations copyright © 1969 by Kurt Werth. All rights reserved. First published in 1969 by The Viking Press, Inc., 625 Madison Avenue, New York, N.Y. 10022. Published simultaneously in Canada by The Macmillan Company of Canada Limited. Library of Congress catalog card number: 76–85868. Printed in U.S.A. by Rae Publishing Co., Inc.
Pic Bk 1. Halloween

©   2   3   4   5   6   74   73   72   71   70
Trade 670–52585–5
VLB 670–52586–3

This is the robber

who came sneaking down the road

one dark night.

This is the ghost

    who came after the robber

    who came sneaking down the road

    one dark night.

This is the witch

who followed the ghost

who came after the robber

who came sneaking down the road

one dark night.

This is the scarecrow

who followed the witch

who followed the ghost

who came after the robber

who came sneaking down the road

one dark night.

This is the skeleton

who followed the scarecrow

who followed the witch

who followed the ghost

who came after the robber

who came sneaking down the road

one dark night.

This is the jack-o'-lantern

    who followed the skeleton

    who followed the scarecrow

    who followed the witch

    who followed the ghost

    who came after the robber

who came sneaking down the road

one dark night.

Sneak . . . sneakery

Squeek . . . squeekery

SQUEEK?

Who said SQUEEK?

What made that SCARY squeek?

UP jumped the robber

    falling back against the ghost

    who fell on the witch

    who fell on the scarecrow

who fell on the skeleton

who fell on the jack-o'-lantern

who ran hooting and hollering right

    back home

followed by the skeleton

pulling the scarecrow

pulling the witch

pulling the ghost

pulling the robber right off his feet.

AND THEY ALL SLAMMED THE DOOR.

And this is the baby mouse

    who came squeeking down the road

    one dark night—

running *squeek squeek squeek squeek*
all the way home.